DATE DUE

FEB 12 2010	
MAR 1 7 2010	
JUL 07 2011	
JUL 2 9 2011	

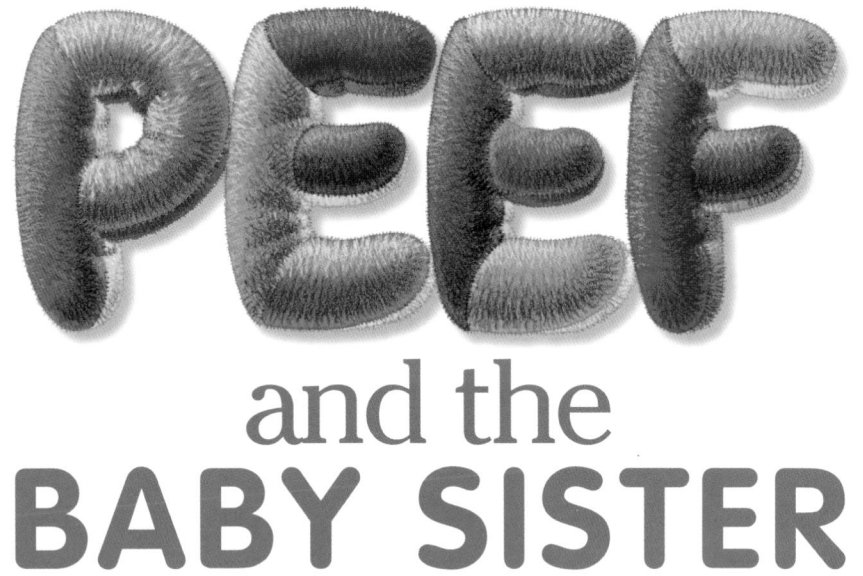

PEEF
and the
BABY SISTER

by Tom Hegg
illustrated by Warren Hanson

Waldman House Press

Minneapolis

For Miss Natalie Haugen
– TH

For Patty and her Sisters
– WH

Library of Congress Cataloging-in-Publication Data
Hegg, Tom.
   Peef and the Baby Sister / by Tom Hegg ; illustrated
by Warren Hanson.
      p. cm.
   Summary: A boy gives his beloved teddy bear and best
friend, Peef, to his new baby sister when nothing else will
comfort her.
   ISBN-13: 978-0-931674-67-9
   ISBN-10: 0-931674-67-0
   [1. Babies – Fiction. 2. Brothers and sisters – Fiction.
   3. Teddy bears – Fiction. 4. Stories in rhyme.]
      I. Hanson, Warren, ill. II. Title.
PZ8.3.H398 Ph 2006
[E] 22   2006042073

Waldman House Press, Inc.
2300 Louisiana Avenue North, Suite B
Golden Valley, MN 55427

Waldman House Press is an imprint of TRISTAN Publishing, Inc.

Please visit us at:
www.waldmanhouse.com

A new adventure always seemed to wait around the bend
For Peef, the multicolored teddy bear and his Best Friend.

They loved to build machines and cities,

fly to Saturn's rings,

And travel Time itself upon imagination's wings.

The years had brought them all the way
from "Candyland" to chess,

But something greater lay in store than they could ever guess.

They heard Mom telling Dad about it
through the bedroom door...

A baby on the way!
The family would soon be four!

Together, they began to wonder what to make of this…
A baby brother, maybe?
Maybe.
Maybe baby sis?

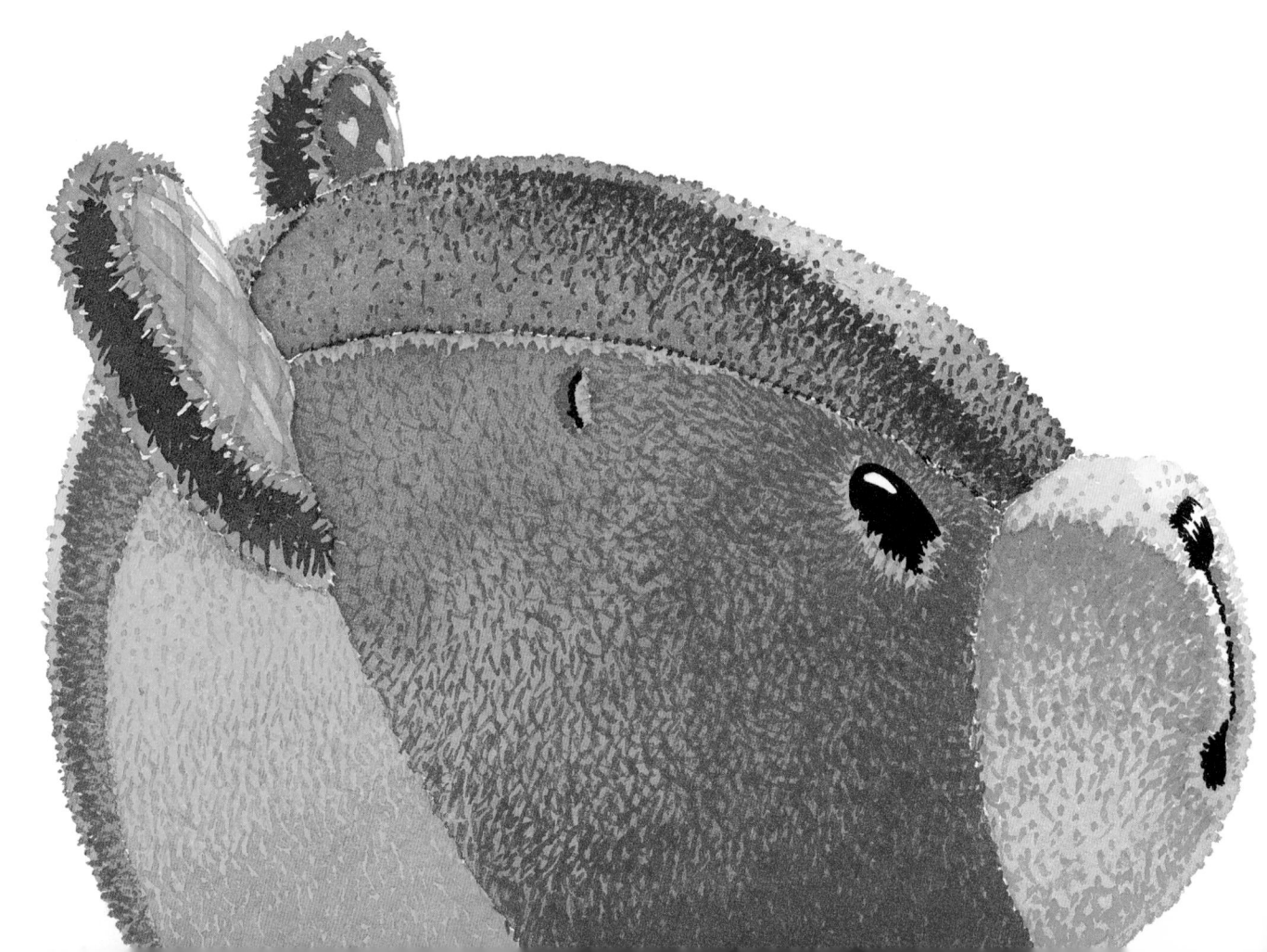

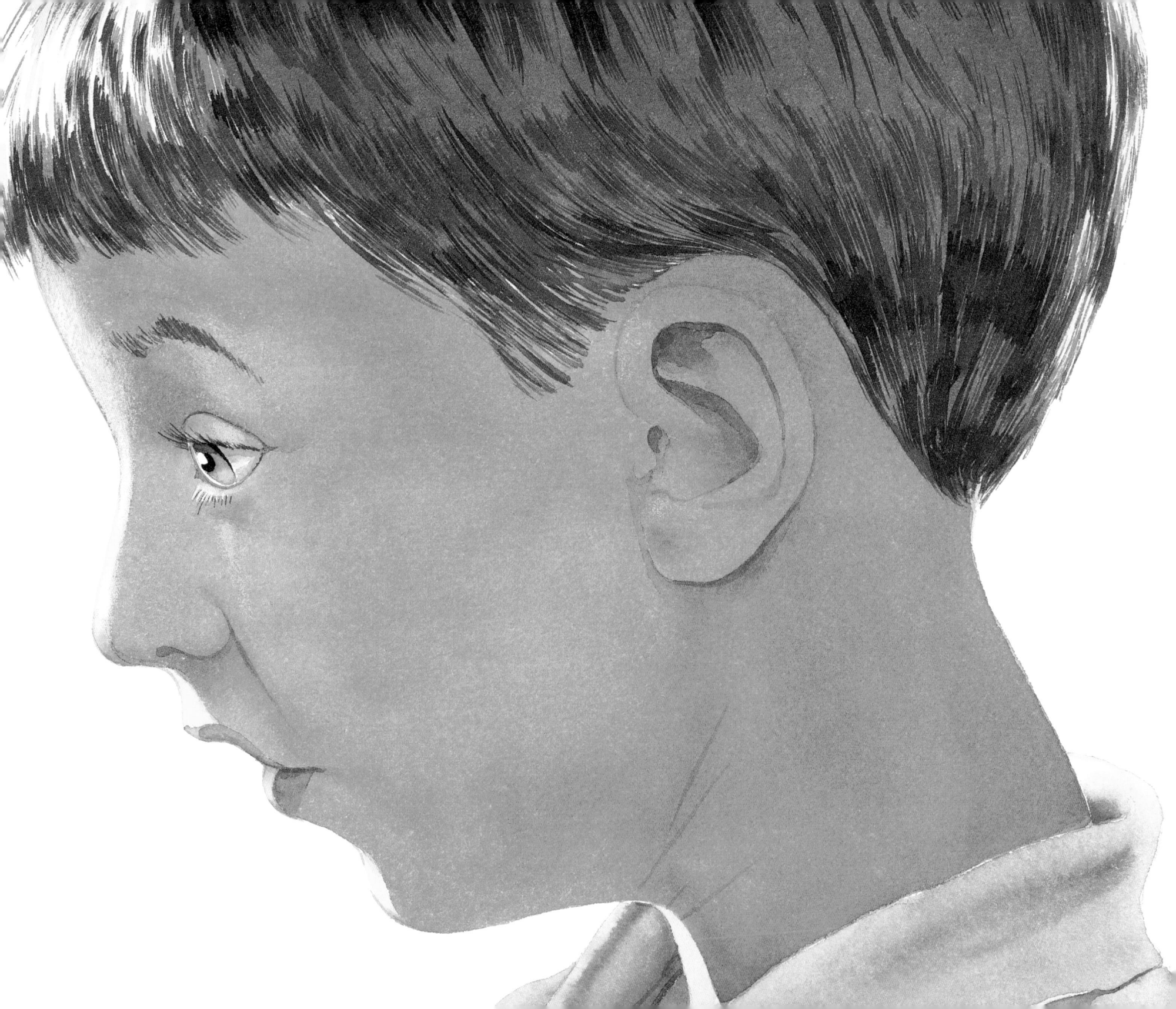

They had to wait a long, long time… and then, one special day,
A baby sister came!

But she was way too small to play.

She cried a lot. She slept a lot. Except when it was night.
It seemed that Mom and Dad were always turning on a light.

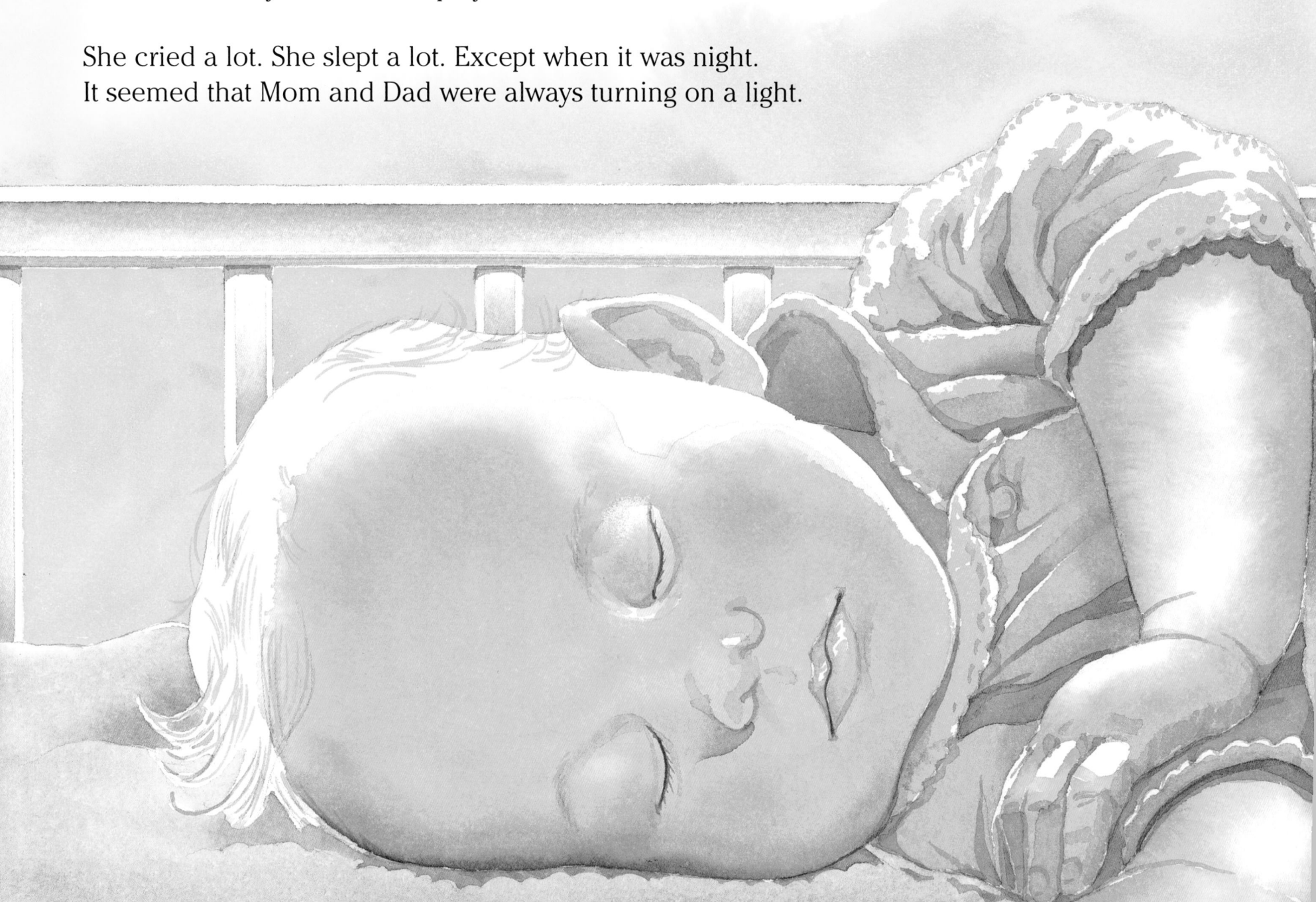

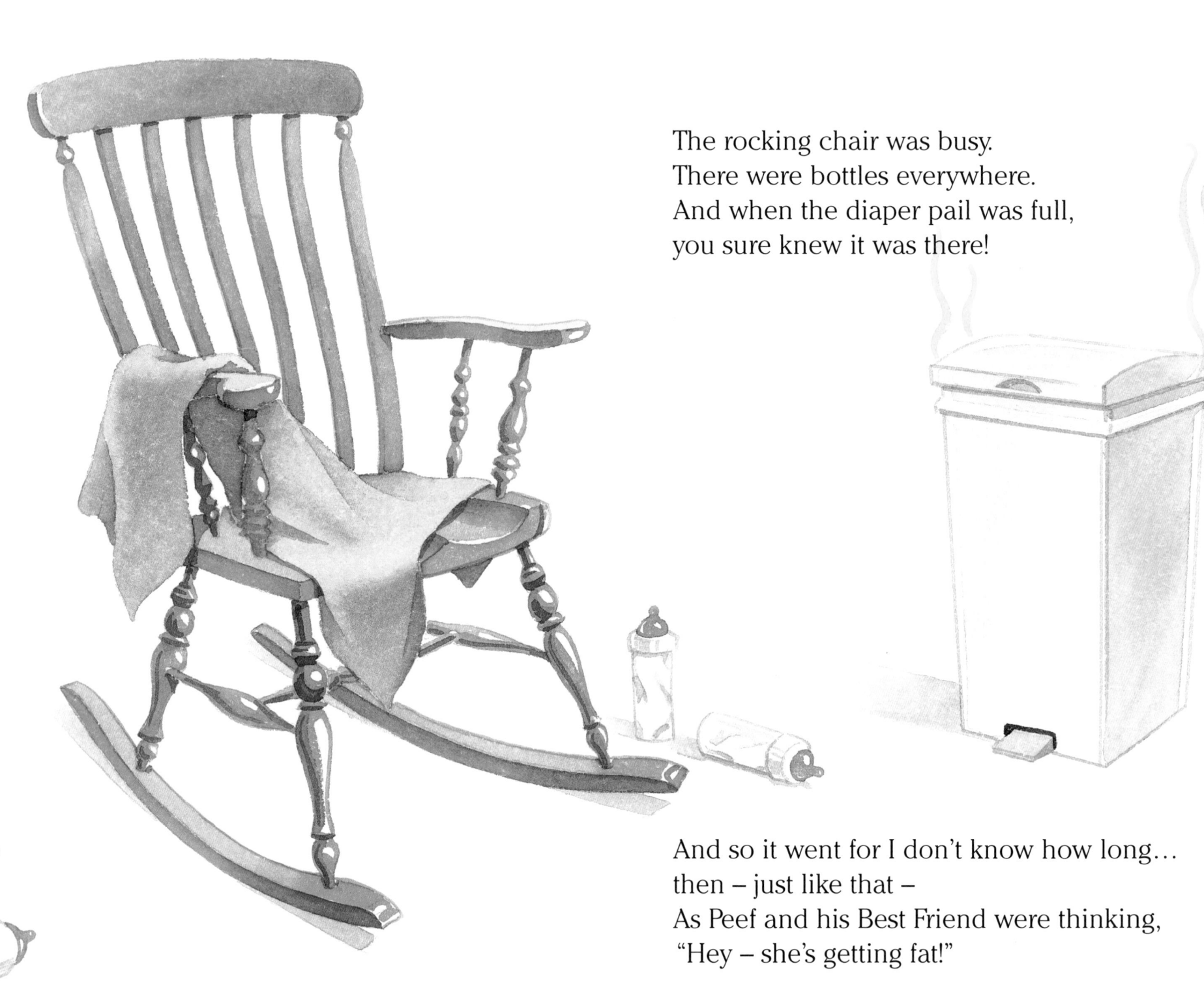

The rocking chair was busy.
There were bottles everywhere.
And when the diaper pail was full,
you sure knew it was there!

And so it went for I don't know how long…
then – just like that –
As Peef and his Best Friend were thinking,
"Hey – she's getting fat!"

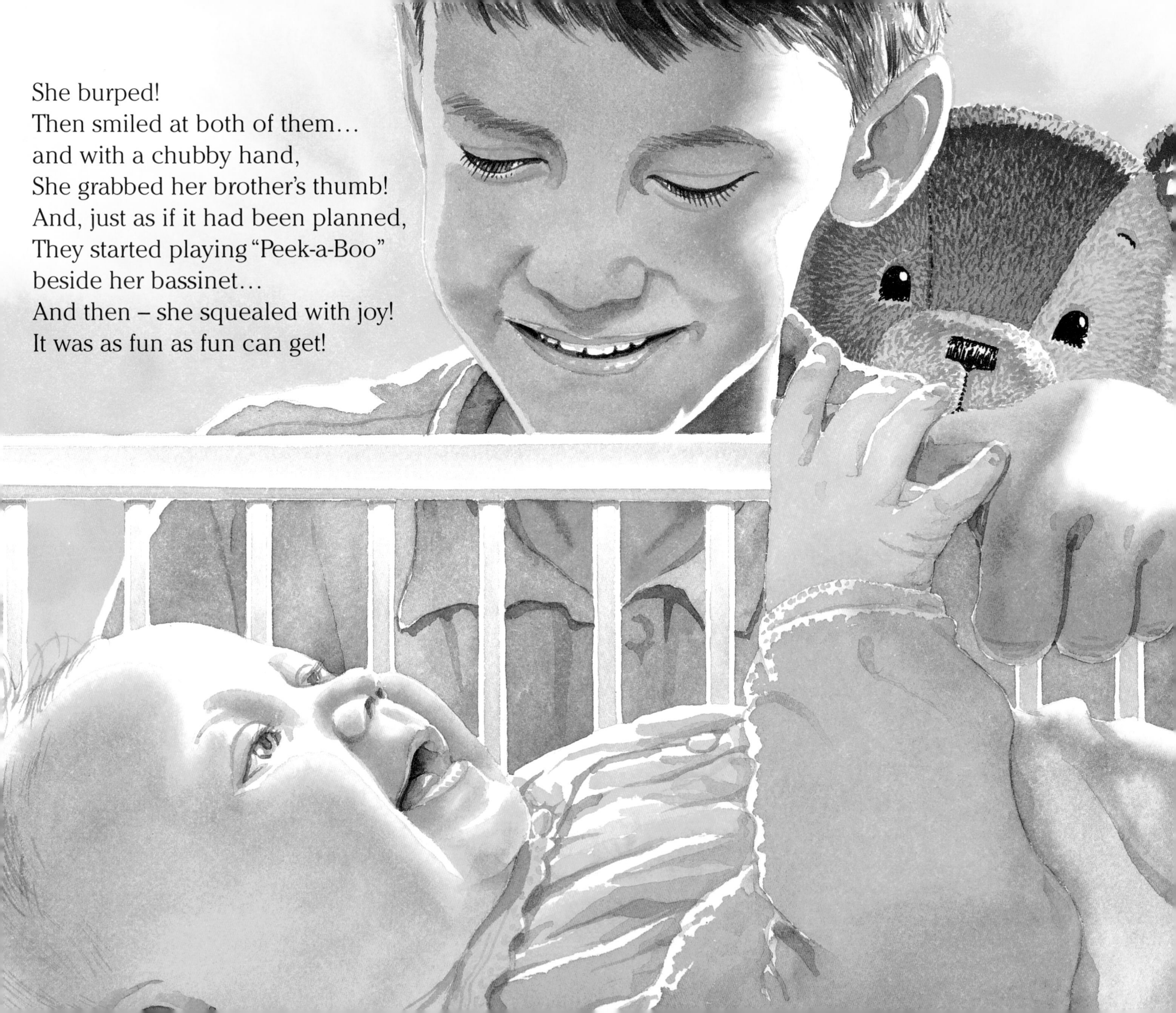

She burped!
Then smiled at both of them…
and with a chubby hand,
She grabbed her brother's thumb!
And, just as if it had been planned,
They started playing "Peek-a-Boo"
beside her bassinet…
And then – she squealed with joy!
It was as fun as fun can get!

But they were only getting started.
Soon, they put on shows

With funny faces.

Magic tricks!

They'd count her tiny toes.

She'd wiggle and she'd clap her hands
and pump her little legs,
And giggle, giggle, giggle
'til they'd both crack up like eggs.

And bit by bit, the teddy bear's Best Friend became, indeed,
The best big brother anyone could ever want – or need.

And then, one day, they heard Mom say,
"She isn't feeling well.
She's not her happy self
because she's teething.
You can tell."

They wondered what to do…

and Peef's Best Friend cried out, "I know!
We'll go and get some stuff
and do a 'feel all better' show!"

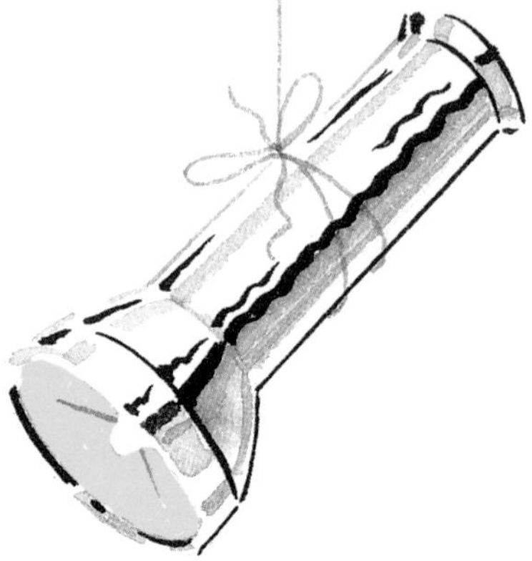

They grabbed a flashlight for a spot,
a dishrag for a cape,
And made – I don't know what –
from toilet paper cores and tape.

They dragged some action figures out from underneath their bed
And posed them all – including one that didn't have a head –
On top of an old skateboard.

Then, they made a big parade
Inside the nursery,
as a kazoo was being played.

Oh, Peef and his Best Friend
did all their very best for her.
The teddy triple-flipped
until he was a fuzzy blur.
They made their funny faces,
sang,
and rode a pogo stick,

They carried on like circus clowns...

but nothing did the trick.

They gathered up the flashlight
and the skateboard
and the toys,
Afraid that they had only made her worse
with all the noise.

They padded back down to their room and slowly shut the door,
And, in the fading light of day…

they sat down on the floor.

The middle of the oval rug
was where they thought their best,
And so, they thought as hard
as if they had to take a test.

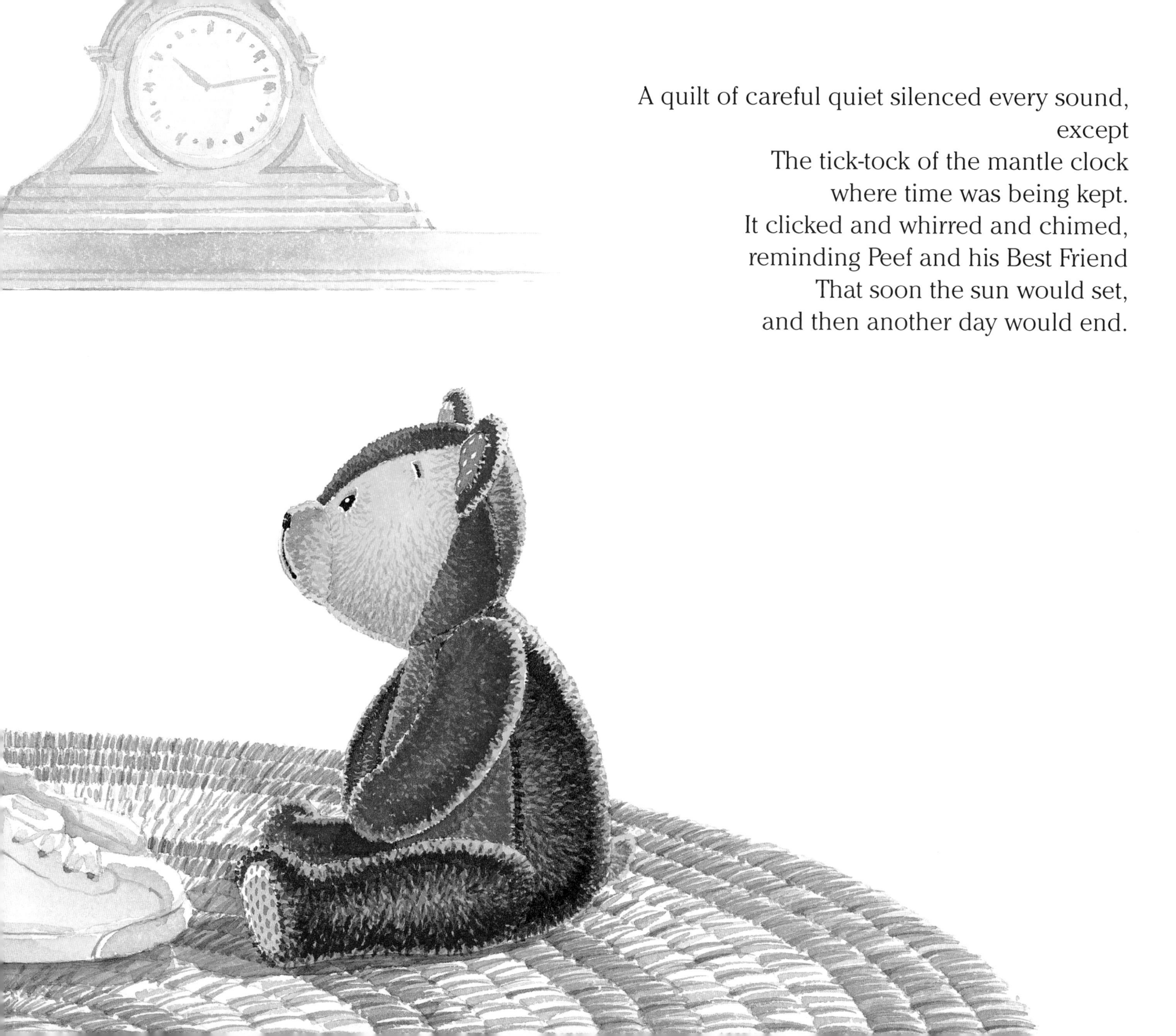

A quilt of careful quiet silenced every sound,
except
The tick-tock of the mantle clock
where time was being kept.
It clicked and whirred and chimed,
reminding Peef and his Best Friend
That soon the sun would set,
and then another day would end.

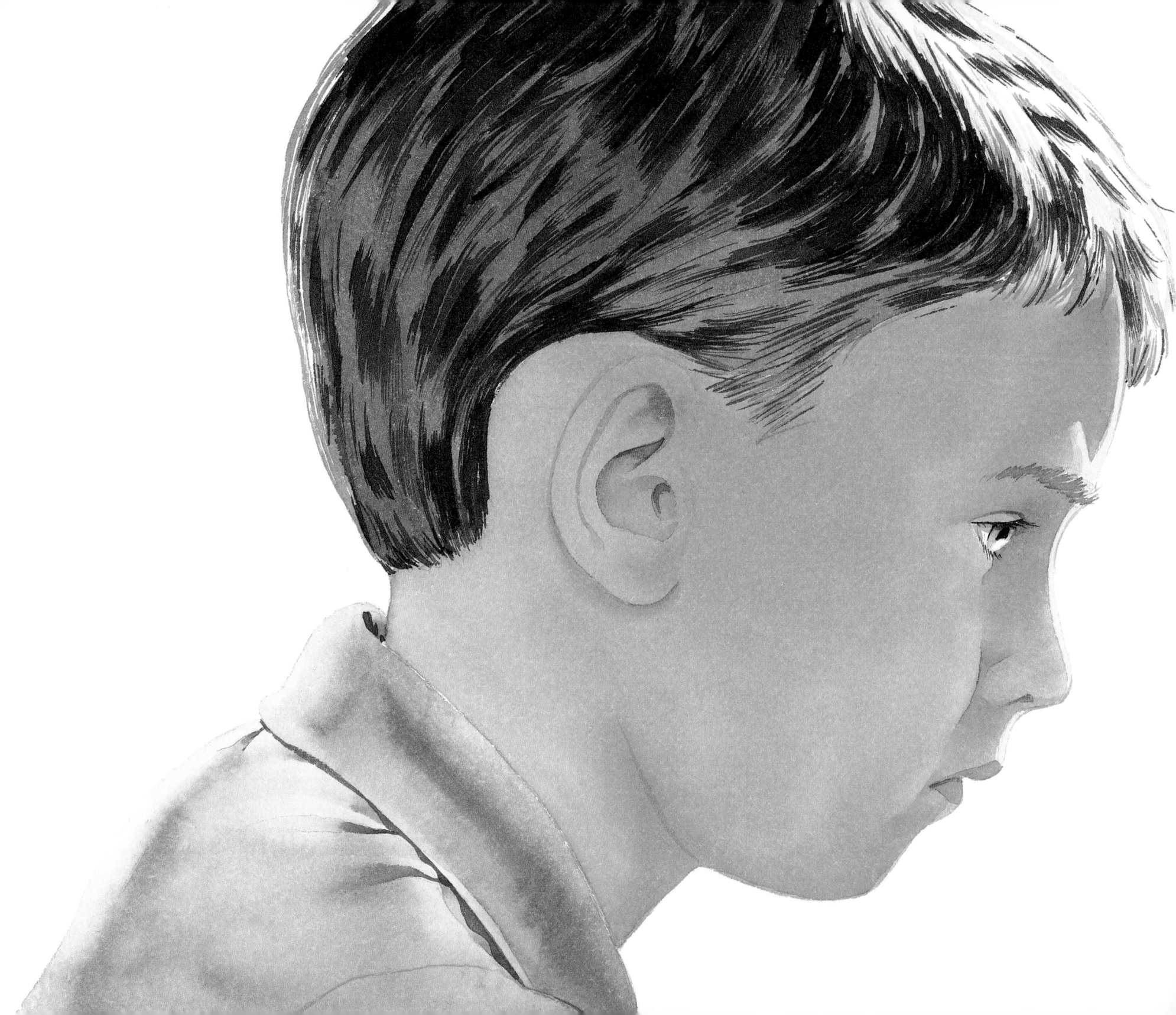

"It all goes by so fast," said Peef.
"You've grown so big and tall.
It seems like you just got those clothes, and look –
they're getting small."

And as the golden light was turning violet and rose,
The teddy said,
"It's time."

They felt a chapter start to close...

And in the early evening glow,
this teddy and this child
Looked up...
and knew what they should do...
and through their tears,
they smiled.

Surrounded by their memories,
upon that oval rug,
The two best friends reached out,

and then they shared one final hug.

They walked into the nursery together, hand in hand,
And then and there, as if,
somehow,
it always had been planned…

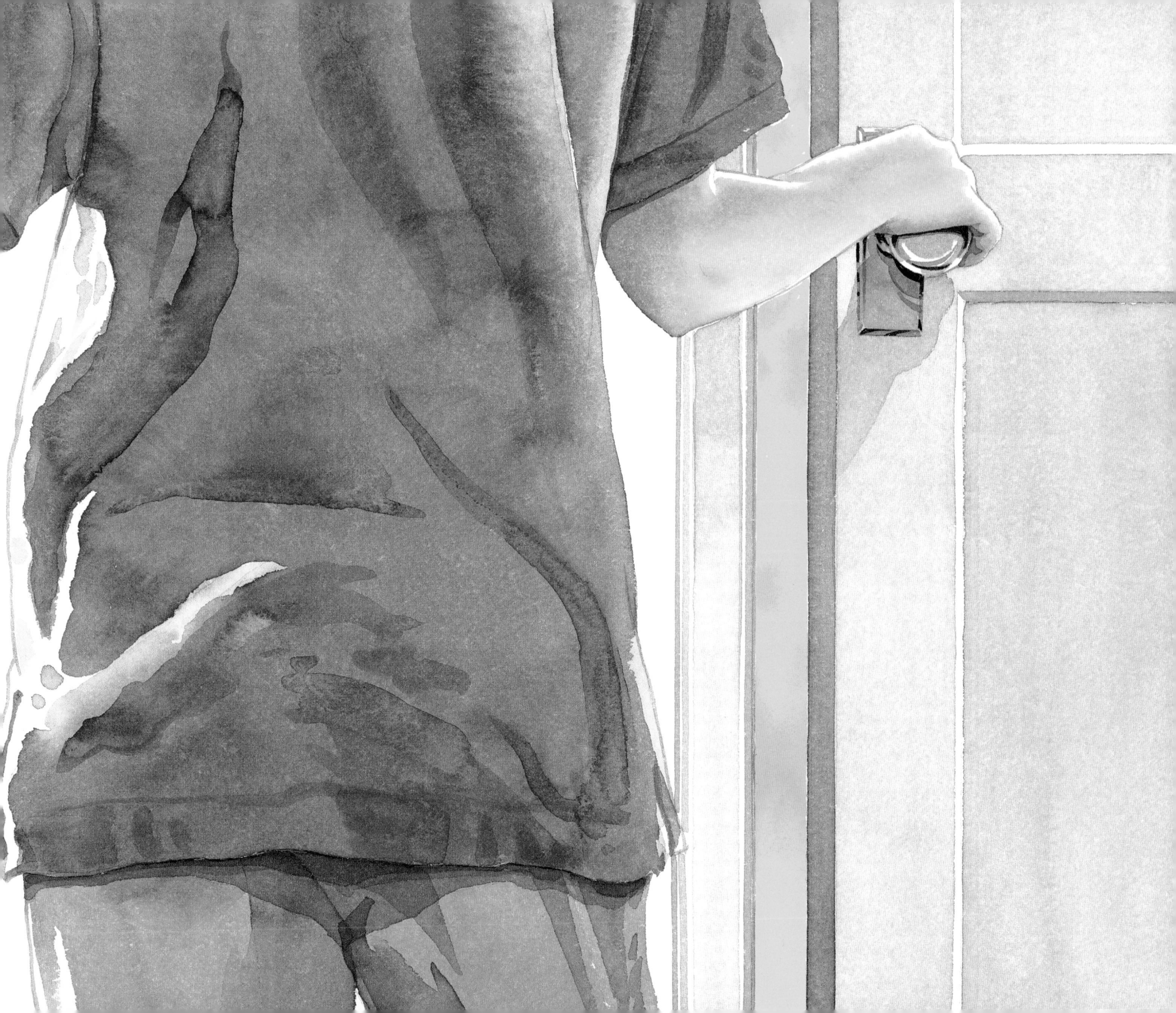

The growing boy picked up the multicolored teddy bear,
And then he said,
"Now all I need to do is touch once… there."

He placed the teddy gently by the baby as she slept,
And felt, deep down inside, as if a promise had been kept.

And as he left, as softly as the turning of a leaf,

He saw his sister smile…
and then, a little bear said, "Peef."